WOMBAT STEW

MARCIA K VAUGHAN
PAMELA LOFTS

A Scholastic Press book from Scholastic Australia

For Mum and Dad with love

Scholastic Press
345 Pacific Highway
Lindfield NSW 2070
An imprint of Scholastic Australia Pty Limited (ABN 11 000 614 577)
PO Box 579
Gosford NSW 2250
www.scholastic.com.au

Part of the Scholastic Group
Sydney • Auckland • New York • Toronto • London • Mexico City
• New Delhi • Hong Kong • Buenos Aires • Puerto Rico

First published by Scholastic Australia in 1984.
This edition published in 2014.
Text copyright © Marcia Vaughan, 1984.
Illustrations copyright © Pamela Lofts, 1984.

National Library of Australia Cataloguing-in-Publication entry

Author:	Vaughan, Marcia K. (Marcia Kay), author.
Title:	Wombat stew / Marcia K Vaughan, author ;
	Pamela Lofts, illustrator.
ISBN:	978-1-74362-257-5 (pbk)
Target Audience:	For pre-school age.
Subjects:	Animals--Australia--Juvenile fiction. Wombats--Juvenile fiction.
	Dingo--Juvenile fiction.
Other Authors/	
Contributors:	Lofts, Pamela, illustrator.
A823.3	

Printed in China by RR Donnelley.

Scholastic Australia's policy, in association with RR Donnelley, is to use papers that
are renewable and made efficiently from wood grown in sustainable forests, so as to
minimise its environmental footprint.

10 9 8 7 6 5 4   16 17 18 / 1

One day, on the banks of a billabong,
a very clever dingo caught a wombat . . .

and decided to make . . .

Wombat stew,
Wombat stew,
Gooey, brewy,
Yummy, chewy,
Wombat stew!

Platypus came ambling up the bank.
'Good day, Dingo,' he said,
snapping his bill.
'What is all that water for?'

'I'm brewing up a gooey, chewy stew with that fat wombat,' replied Dingo with a toothy grin.

'If you ask me,' said Platypus,
'the best thing for a gooey stew is mud.
Big blops of billabong mud.'

'Blops of mud?' Dingo laughed.
'What a good idea.
Righto, in they go!'

So Platypus scooped up big blops
of mud with his tail and tipped
them into the billycan.

Around the bubbling billy,
Dingo danced and sang . . .

'Wombat stew,
Wombat stew,
Gooey, brewy,
Yummy, chewy,
Wombat stew!'

Waltzing out from the shade of the ironbarks came Emu. She arched her graceful neck over the brew.

'Oh ho, Dingo,' she fluttered.
'What have we here?'

'Gooey, chewy wombat stew,'
boasted Dingo.

'If only it were a bit more chewy,'
she sighed. 'But don't worry.
A few feathers will set it right.'

'Feathers?' Dingo smiled.
'That would be chewy!
Righto, in they go!'

So into the gooey brew
Emu dropped
her finest feathers.

Around and around
the bubbling billy,
Dingo danced and sang . . .

'Wombat stew,
Wombat stew,
Crunchy, munchy,
For my lunchy,
Wombat stew!'

Old Blue Tongue the Lizard
came sliding off his sun-soaked stone.

'*Sss*illy Dingo,' he hissed.
'There are no flies*ss* in this *sss*tew.
Can't be wombat *sss*tew
without crunchy flies*ss* in it.'
    And he stuck out
        his bright blue tongue.

'There's a lot to be said for flies,'
agreed Dingo, rubbing his paws together.

'Righto, in they go!'

So Lizard snapped
one hundred flies from the air
with his long tongue and flipped them
into the gooey, chewy stew.

Around and around and around
the bubbling billy,
Dingo danced and sang . . .

'Wombat stew,
Wombat stew,
Crunchy, munchy,
For my lunchy,
Wombat stew!'

Up through the red dust popped Echidna.
'Wait a bit. Not so fast,' he bristled, shaking the
red dust from his quills.

'Now, I've been listening to all this advice –
and take it from me, for a munchy stew you need
slugs and bugs and creepy crawlies.'

Dingo wagged his tail.
'Why, I should have thought of that.
Righto, in they go!'

So Echidna dug up all sorts of creepy crawlies and dropped them into the gooey, chewy, crunchy stew.

The very clever Dingo stirred and stirred,
all the while singing . . .

'Wombat stew,
Wombat stew,
Hot and spicy,
Oh so nicey,
Wombat stew!'

Just then the sleepy-eyed Koala
climbed down the scribbly gumtree.

'Look here,' he yawned,
'any bush cook knows you can't make
a spicy stew without gumnuts.'

'Leave it to a koala to think of gumnuts,'
Dingo laughed and licked his whiskers.

'Righto, in they go!'

And into the gooey, chewy, crunchy, munchy stew
Koala shook lots and lots of gumnuts.

'Ah ha!' cried Dingo.
'Now my stew is missing only one thing.'

'What's that?' asked the animals.

'That fat wombat!'

'Wait!'

'Stop!'

'Hang on, Dingo!
You can't put that wombat
into the stew yet.'

'Why not?'

'You haven't tasted it.'

'Righto! I'll taste it!'

And that very clever dingo
bent over the billy
and took a great, big slurp of stew.

'I'm poisoned!' he howled.
'You've all tricked me!'

And he dashed away
deep into the bush,
never again to sing . . .

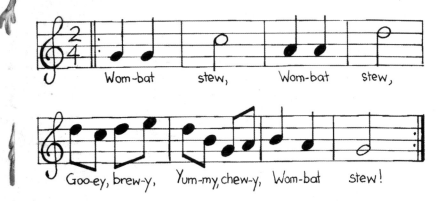

Wom-bat stew, Wom-bat stew,

Goo-ey, brew-y, Yum-my, chew-y, Wom-bat stew!

'Wombat stew,
Wombat stew,
Gooey, brewy,
Yummy, chewy,
Wombat stew!'